TEN WEEKS THAT CHANGED ENGLAND

She is just a woman in the milling crowd
Westminster and what she hears first is
horses' hoofs on the cobblestones as the
street from the Horse Ferry. The roar a
clash of steel, of armour, of swords rattling in scabbards, and ...
shouts of the captains, the combined response of the militia
increases until it is a deafening wave of sound and then she sees
them, the duke's men, his cavalcade sweeping by on the way to the
opening of Parliament, black horses tossing their heads against the
restraint of harness, clipped manes plaited and beribboned in green
and gold, coats polished to the brightness of mirrors, riders like
enamelled toys, everything spruce and rich and glittering as it
flashes by and she sees in the great press of horse flesh, man
flesh, royal power, in sunlight harsh before rain, with the shadow
of the great tower briefly like a hand passing over the men, the
horses, she sees them riding through this shadow, and in the midst
of the roar and glitter she sees him, John of Gaunt, the duke of
Lancaster, the puissant duke, surrounded by his close body-guard
armed to the teeth, their shining casques, their breast-plates,
cuirasses, greaves, all accoutred and fearsome to the unarmed,
thread-bare, unshod populace, and a foul threat to those who oppose
this ancient force, this arrogation of power and, as if oblivious to
it, he, the great duke, the third son, Head of the King's Council,
stares straight ahead between the ears of his war horse, face set in
disdain for the lower orders, the populace, the populists, the
rabble, the stink and heat of them closing in on both sides of his
cavalcade, held back, held in place, pressed back where they belong,
by the armed guards, by the guards of the great duke, his disdain
expressed in a baleful stare, even his combed and powdered beard
expressing contempt in its perfection, its order, like his garments
of triple-dyed velvet, slashed sleeves revealing purple silk
slithering next to his skin, his ducal skin, his royal skin, and on
his feet his riding boots of Spanish leather, his gold spurs, and on
his hands his rings, his rings glinting on every finger, his
Plantagenet fingers, and his chain of office, this office impressive
to anyone below the rank of king, this third son, this malcontent

despite his lucrative marriages bringing lands to rival those of his father, Edward the King of England, and now he, assuming the power of his dying, beloved and fabled elder brother known in later times as the Black Prince, the magnificent prince, the war hero, this duke now, John, beringed, puissant, riding his war horse towards Parliament in the year thirteen hundred and seventy six, expresses disdain and the crowd falls silent as he and his army roar past.

The woman in the crowd watches him go.

He is the most hated man in England. Hated for his rapacity, his many mistresses, for the shameless exploitation of his female servants and the numberless children fathered on them, hated because he schemed his way to what he is now, Head of the King's Council, the chief in council, powerful now that the venerable yet senile King Edward III is too weak to hold the sceptre in his grip. He is hated for allowing corruption at court, for allowing the hard-earned money of the over-taxed poor to be squandered on failed and humiliating battles with the French in a war nobody but the nobles want, he is hated for allowing the courtesan Alice Perrers free access to the royal jewels, the pearls, the gold, the rubies and to filch coin from the king's coffers which are filled with all that stolen from the people, from people taxed into starvation, stoical people who till the land, who grow the crops, who breed the animals, who run the Guilds that make every single object of use and beauty this realm is capable of producing, all these, the people of England, exploited and disdained by such as he, this duke, riding to Parliament to exact yet more pence from a people who can no longer pay for the bread to feed their children, and hated, this stand-in for the old magnificent fake, the old king, for allowing these riches accrued in war and by the labour of the people to be squandered to satisfy the passing fads of court sycophants and the greedy and ambitious nobility, the dukes, the earls, the barons.

This woman in the crowd watches him ride by.

And so the thundering uproar of his cavalcade drowns out the silence of the citizens of London and the folk from the shires as it has always drowned out the silence of the powerless. The duke believes he has a God-given right to do so. Only one voice is allowed and it is not that of the people. It will not be the voice of the people. It will never be so. And yet he is riding to the parliament when, they say, the voice of the people will be heard. It must be heard. The shire knights and the city merchants demand it. Compassion for the poor and starving demands it. Righteousness demands it. Justice demands it. The weak and mild and servile at last demand it. It is their right. The Commons will speak for them. This time they will speak and this time they will be heard.

The cacophony of horses and riders continues over the silence of the crowd herded behind the lines of guards, it continues, as it seems, without end until something changes. Something happens. It is so sudden it seems like a miracle and a reversion of all the laws of reason. It is a black miracle.

It has the power to make the double lines of horses falter, like a break in the forward surge of a wave, like an ocean's ripple of coming storm, disturbing the disciplined ranks, the metallic power of the passing militia because, unplanned, unexpected, a child - it is a child, a girl with streaming hair - this child runs out under the linked arms of the armed guards posted along the route to protect the duke and all the upholders of privilege, this child runs under the arms, under the gauntlets and the raised swords, and the guards only see her when she is already alongside Gaunt's destrier, his big war horse caparisoned in blue silk threaded with gold and embroidered in the symbols of his House of Lancaster, they only see her when she calls up to him, her face turned up as a flower to the sun, and when she falls under the hoofs of his horse and when the blood pours down the side of her head they see her then and the crowd gasps and presses forward with an anger risen suddenly in a hot eruption at this further insult to their humanity because Gaunt, the great duke, seeing the child, seeing her fall and seeing the blood, rides on, he rides on, and his men after him and the child lies still as they thunder past.

It has taken a moment, a blink of an eye but, quickly following, a figure in a black robe pushes through the guards with peremptory confidence and, by virtue of her Benedictine habit the guards give way and she runs to the child, bending to cradle her, to succour her, to weep. She is followed by the woman from out of the crowd who has watched in silence as the duke rides by, a woman attired in the expensive garments worn by the wife of a shire knight, in crimson cloth, miniver-trimmed, her hair loose beneath its fillet,

3

glittering silver pale to her waist, her cloak for a moment
concealing the child from the onlookers who were standing near and
who are now pressing against the guards, oblivious of swords and
menaces, the soldiers' curses, and as the cavalcade clatters on in
its arrogance and bustle to the yard in front of Westminster Hall
and the guards, job done, their lord safely dismounting and entering
the great hall, follow on, leaving the way free for the crowd to
press towards the fallen child as others, streaming in the wake of
the guards, begin to mill like packed wolves outside the iron-
studded doors of the Great Hall, this woman from among the onlookers runs forward to aid the nun. Guards, swords crossed,
prevent access to the parliament hall and stare straight through the
faces of the people as if they cannot see them, through those men
and women jostling a raging but prudent blade length away with their
anger curling before them. And the law of deference prevails.

But the group round the child are noisy, indignant. They heard
her plea to Gaunt. Help me, your Grace, we are hungry. Please help
us, I beg you, for the sake of my little brother and sister, we are
hungry. Please give them something to eat.

And she fell in front of him. Did he lash out at her?

I wouldn't put it past him.

I didn't see. Did you?

How could he hurt her? A mere child!

What else do you expect?

He rode on!

Arrogance. Too high for remorse.

Hatred for all his breed. The Lord will punish him in
hell.

Or we will pull him down the sooner.

The child, a girl of no more than eight is lying
motionless on the ground with the Benedictine nun wiping
her bruised and bloody forehead with her sleeve. The
woman in the crowd with the silvery skein of hair, reaches
inside her cloak and pulls out a linen cloth to staunch
the blood. We must take her somewhere where we can attend
to her, she says.

4

The nun agrees. Help me carry her into the abbey. The monks in the hospitium will help us.

The lady calls, Guy! We need your strength. A handsome youth of about eighteen wearing the ivory and green colours of his lord, slouches forward. Ever willing, dear lady sister. Bending to lift the child he gently crooks the little bag of bones with its tousled hair and cheap hempen frock into his arms and the small group, followed as far as the abbey precinct, is watched by the silent crowd as they take her inside to safety.

Two children trail after them like little lost table dogs, one a boy of six or so blubbing loudly dragging with him a silent tottering girl of two or three. They are emaciated. Nothing but bone, the sharp joints almost sticking through their flesh, unkempt hair a fuzz like birds' nests, a red sore on the boy's mouth. They attach themselves to the group tending the injured girl. They stand like shadows in the doorway of the hospitium and nobody thinks to usher them away.

Eventually the boy presses his knuckles into his eyes to repress his tears and bravely steps close enough to tug at the edge of a cloak. My lady? and when the lady turns he steps back as if expecting a blow and she notes his distress, his frightened face, his eyes darting and fixing on the white face of the other child lying prostrate in blood on the stone flags.

What is it, young master?

It's our Bet you've got there.

Is she your sister?

He nods. Tears flood his eyes. She's our mother now our real mother's dead. He begins to howl with a sudden, unrestrained grief he is unable to cage into words while the baby, the toddler, gripping tightly to the torn hem of his tunic, her tiny knuckles white, like seed pearls,

5

stands mute with eyes wide enough to take in all the
horror of her brother's grief and the as yet unfelt grief
of her own orphaned world.

The helpful esquire in his smart town clothes turns from
the nun and the cloaked woman and goes over to the two
children. He crouches to their level. They'll fix her up,
he consoles. Worry not. The monks will make her as good
as new.

As if shocked at being spoken to in such soft tones the
boy stops his howling on a gulp and stares like a cornered
sparrow, backing away, dragging the small child with him,
to huddle against the wall, fluttering and trapped. The
esquire begins to rummage under his cloak.

Here, have something to drink, my little chicks. He
unties a leather bottle from off his belt and holds it
out. The boy looks on longingly but make no move to take
it. The toddler glances at him, glances back at the gift,
almost reaches out but then, courage failing, hides her
face in her brother's sleeve.

Come now, my sister-in-law wishes it, he persuades,
turning towards the woman in the cloak who is now in
urgent conversation with the hospitaller. He waits until
she is finished then calls softly, Hildegard, look at
these two waifs here, what do we do with them?

The nun is already following the injured child where she
is being carried on a small stretcher into the hospitium.
A monk instructs his assistant on how to tend her
injuries. The two children watch their sister being taken
away. They stand like small wooden statues in the
doorway. Other monks appear as the esquire pushes the
bottle into the boy's hand who, mastering his fear,
snatches it up and drinks until he chokes then holds it
out for his little sister, guiding it to her mouth while
the lady is offering to pay the nuns, the monks, for their

care of the injured child. The little one drinks and gulps and drinks again. Noticing the two urchins in the doorway one of the monks offers a kindly smile and shepherds them over the threshold until like lambs in sudden eager pursuit of a ewe, they rush ahead of him into the echoing building to follow their sister and he murmurs after them: all will be well, all will be well, and all will ever be well amen.

When everything is settled, the esquire, Guy, and his sister-in-law, Hildegard, step into the sunlit yard and are sucked at once into the thick of the crowd gathering with increasing force outside the parliament hall. Anger hangs like a miasma over their heads - so thick you can cut it, murmurs the squire - as the crowds press in to watch more nobles arrive, weapons burnished and glimmering through the moist April light, the cavalcades continually sweeping aside the bystanders who in a listing of names, of hated names identify the newcomers, Latimer, Lyons and their retinues, and when they are safely past let their words fly free.

Demanding our money again for their wars. Why not suck our blood direct and have done with it? God curse them.

It's us forced to recoup Gaunt's losses. Why should we? It's his war, his loss, not ours. A plague on the man.

A litany of recent defeats follows yet again. Everyone knows them off by heart.

These battles, engaged and lost, occurred in real places. Places across the Narrow Seas in a foreign country, in France, in Flanders, where people much like themselves had to suffer the rapacious attacks of foreign mercenaries on their land and property but yet, in these end years of King Edward's reign and despite the victories at Crecy, Poitiers, when his army won against the odds and started to see themselves as English, the combined forces of the French dukes are now managing to beat them off. Everyone here knows the names of the leaders of these present humiliations and almost to the penny they know how much it costs each one of them in taxes and fines and, if unpaid, of time spent in prison, and yet how much it costs can be calculated in less gross terms than gold, than in taxes, and is more accurately computed in the measure of grief and loss of hope, the unassuaged pain of loved ones, of lost self-esteem and they know that they, the people, suffer on both sides. Where are the victories? they ask. Why are we fighting our brothers and sisters across the Narrow Seas? Where is our quarrel with them? Everyone knows the expensive defeats off by heart. Where is the respite? they ask. When will it end? And most heart-felt of all they ask, after these taxes where is the bread to feed our children?

The young man, Guy, who carried the girl into the abbey hospital, rests a comforting hand on the shoulder of his sister-in-law. Don't look so distressed, Hildegard. We've done what we can.

It is not enough, Guy...I have been immured in comfort in my Welsh idyll so long that the world of cities, of London, of the outside, of the nobles attacks across the seas has made me dull. What I see around me here in London is too shocking to take in all at once. Such poverty everywhere. How do the people survive?

Just then the crowd surges forward as a horn heralds the approach of someone else of importance arriving at the opening - is it the King himself? - people at the back stand on tiptoe to catch a glimpse, sure he will save them from the greed of his third son but then they see a line of drummers coming into view followed by a glittering gold palanquin visible above their heads as if floating in the empyrean with the glory of its burden, and silence folds itself over the surging crowd, under the clamour of the drums and pipes, a silence from the onlookers broken only by a few jeers, a repressed catcall, and over their heads Hildegard glimpses a figure in a golden gown with a glittering coronet on her rippling hair, borne briskly along on a litter supported on the shoulders of six silken-cloaked youths, everything about this spectacle suggesting a female deity from the ancient days, an Aphrodite, a Minerva, or a Medusa perhaps, with snaking blonde locks, and everything golden, the gown, the hair, the settings for the flashing jewels on every finger and the great egg of a balas ruby resting in its golden nest on her bosom, everything, even her slippers of gold thread delicate as something spun from spider webs, suggesting gold and wealth and power and of course she is smiling despite the frost glittering in the eyes of those who behold her, those in their drab and fustian and with hungry bellies and in their arms their pale and famished children.

The Lady of the Sun, growls an onlooker close by in derision.

Lady my arse, his companion replies. Lady with-her-hand-in-our-pockets more like.

One hand in our pockets and the other in the King's privy parts. That's her.

Ragged children press between the forest of legs belonging to their elders to get close enough to witness this fantastic apparition. They are stunned. Is it real? Is she a living being? Does she cough and shit like them? A baby, oblivious to this glitter and show, wearing nothing but a ragged blanket howls in its mother's arms and, grime-stained, she presses her wasted cheek against

9

its own for comfort but without able to stem its hungry cries. Has anybody got a crust to spare? she asks fretfully. For the love of God, somebody?

The stranger who made the comment about the Lady of the Sun opens his pouch and brings out a small, squashed pie. Here, take it, my dear, and St Margaret bless you.

The woman grabs his hand with her free one and covers it in kisses. There are tears standing in her eyes. The grace of God on you, sir.

Where's your man when you need him?

Waiting on that accursed war to start up again, she replies breaking off a piece of crust and holding it to the mouth of her infant. The baby clutches it in both small fists and crams it between its tiny lips, eyes closing in bliss, and the woman longingly and regretfully lets it take all.

No need for that, my lass. The stranger extracts a penny from his pouch. Feed yourself, the better to be strong for your babe.

Hildegard watches this small scene and guesses that it is being repeated many times over in the streets and alleyways of this over-flowing city. Coming from the West and on this, her first day in the capital, she and her esquire have so far only penetrated the suburb of Westminster, and even though it is a place with many grand houses where members of the court make their living and accrue their wealth, a place where the Church is the great centre of life, here as in heaven the mirror of government and the place where parliament is about to be opened by the King, she fears to imagine what the commercial centre will be like, the City of London behind its massive stone walls, with its teeming populace struggling to make a living and the merchants restive against the barons and traders from the vast world across the seas homing in on its honey pot like a swarm of bees seeking the hive, and she fears to imagine it further than this, with its heap of unkindness pile on pile, like bones, like death.

Even in her castle in the Welsh Marches near Penarlag she has heard of Newgate, the debtors' prison and the whole hot weight of need and poverty and despair presses down on her spirits now, with the girl flinging herself on Gaunt's mercy, with the young woman and the baby, with the stench of poverty everywhere she looks and she thinks of the mild green of the Welsh hills of her adopted home, of the sheep on the hillside, the wool yields, the great hall with its singing and good cheer and its tables of plenty, the rise of the sun and the falling of soft rain and the harmony of a people well-fed and safe so long as King Edward does not rear up from his sick bed and start another brutal war with the princes, the descendants of Madog ap Gruffudd and the sons of Llewllyn the Last.

She turns to her brother-in-law. Did you really look carefully at those three children, Guy? They are beggars. They are in rags. They are nothing but skin and bone. Without shoes. Without anything. The smallest child, the silent one, could have been no more than four. And the one who ran into the road, she said they'd been forced to sleep under the wharfs ever since their mother died from the plague months since and their father gone they know not where. The child said, I make a little nest for my brother and sister and we curl up together quite snug and much warmer than at first now winter's over. No more than babies, Guy. It breaks my heart. What is to become of them?

The nuns will care for them. You heard what the Sister said. Why did they not seek help before?

They're children. How could they know what to do?

He sighs. The palanquin in its luxury of stolen wealth passes by leaving only the echo of drum-beats and a shrill whining final blast of the horn.

Be it so, she tells him when the sound dies, I shall go back and see what else I might do for them.

We have other business first. That's why we're here.

I am not likely to forget. She looks him directly in the eyes. Do you think I'm likely to forget?

After the dignitaries have entered the hall where the barons are to hold their deliberations as soon as the king arrives to open the proceedings the people, locked out, begin to disperse and plan when to return. There is much ribald singing in the streets. Gangs of youths set up chants against the court and are scattered, shouting and bellicose, by bailiffs with ready cudgels. The neighbour who accompanied the lady Hildegard from her Welsh redoubt rejoins her in the abbey yard. He bends his head. Kisses the back of her hand. Straightens. A smile on his lips but not in his eyes.

My gracious lady, are you intent on staying with the nuns as Guy informs me?

My lord John, she replies with matched formality, you well know I cannot accept your hospitality without compromising my widowhood.

You will remarry. I trust your choice will fall on me. Heaven forfend I should pre-empt your decision by an accusation of abduction?

I would be horrified if you imagined I would suspect you of such base intentions, my lord.

She casts a sidelong glance at her brother-in-law.

Guy, you will accompany me to the guest house in the abbey and then send word to Sir John when I am safely lodged.

And we meet on the morrow to lodge your plea with the clerk-at-law, he concludes tendentiously. Sir John kisses her hand once more before leaving.

Today is the twenty-eighth day of April in the year of our lord thirteen hundred and seventy-six. Hildegard has been escorted over the long miles to London by this neighbour, a minor knight from the Welsh borders who has an eye on her land now she is about to declare herself a widow. She is twenty-two. Her children, Bertrand who is five and two-year old Ysabella are at home in the castle near Penarlag with their nurse maids and the damozels of the chamber. She misses the children already but is preparing herself for an even greater loss when they are placed in other households at the usual age and she will be forced to give them into the care of others. Her thoughts stop here in fright. She does not wish to lose them but she wishes to do her best for them. She is told it is best for a child to be brought up by others so that it quickly learns self-reliance and how to behave to its greater advantage in the adult world and, besides, they are wards of the king now her husband is dead. She has no choice.

My poor babies, she says, over and over, poor babies, poor little ones, my poor nestlings. But the time is not yet. There is the immediate future to settle first, the reason she is here in Westminster, the reason for her meeting with a clerk-at-law who will present her case for judgement and - her thoughts coil back to the problems that lie ahead and she sits down beside Guy and says, tomorrow, when I make application to the court for control of Hugh's lands until Bertrand comes of age, I may be refused. They may not accept the evidence of his death. They may say it is premature, that his disappearance is

13

temporary, that the evidence for death is poor. Or, accepting it, I may be allotted my third from the estate and sent packing, landless yet prey to men set on marrying a dowered widow. My life will change completely. I can think no further than tomorrow.

If she is denied the property near Penarlag she considers returning to her own people in Yorkshire. This is a dream and indistinct. It is, to be honest, a dream of childhood. Of running around Castle Hutton being chased by the head woodsman's teasing son, Ulf, and being taught how to shoot a straight arrow by him, and how to fight to defend herself, for we live in turbulent times, he tells her, a serious youth of fourteen at this time of her dreaming, and I will not always be by to protect you, but this is a dream she dare not stare at too long in case its emptiness overwhelms her. Ulf has grown up to become Lord Roger's steward since she was sent away to be married and she last saw him standing bare-headed in the rain outside the walls of Castle Hutton as, with the gap widening between them, she rode her little grey horse beside her betrothed towards her privileged and uncertain future.

She is aware that if her status as widow of Sir Hugh de Ravenscroft is entered as a plea and accepted, pray that it is, her life might go on as it did when Hugh was sent to France to fight in Arundel's army, when she became used to her husband's comings and goings, his brief returns, bloodied, looking for succour, or triumphant and loaded with the spoils of war, leaving her as chatelaine when, during all those years, she made the day to day decisions on the running of the estate with the help of old Gwylim ap Gwylim, steward borne where he now lives in the castle on the hill and from the first her trusted go-between with the shepherds who tended the sheep and brought in the staple.

She confesses all this to her young brother-in-law, adding, my wish is for Gwylim so to continue until Bertrand comes into his patrimony and I retire with my dower into comfortable old age. You know this, Guy. I know what you fear. You are not disinherited. I wish you to stay, to help as you have always done. It is your home. Nothing has changed. Nothing will change whatever happens to me.

He goes off later to talk to some Welsh bowmen he spotted in the crowd earlier that day and returns later after Compline to tell her that Sir John, red as a turkey cock, was unable to conceal his rage at her reluctance to accept his hospitality. Why has she chosen to be a guest of strangers? he demanded of me. You know he prides himself on his looks and his attractiveness to women, Guy mocked. And you are aware of that too, Hildegard, he added slyly, because I've seen you looking at him when you think no-one is watching.

Again she repeats to Guy what they all very well know. If she is discovered to have spent a night under Sir John's roof her status would be compromised and a marriage contract assumed. Should that happen she would lose everything to her so-called husband. That is the law. That is how it is done in these days when men make the law. Many women fall foul of being abducted. It is called *raptus*. It is written in the law books. The lesser the heiress, the less her danger. Even so. The fact is their lands adjoin, together they would be a force to complement the Mortimer and Talbot lords in the south on behalf of the king. She is aware of that. She is not a fool. Even so, she repeats, I will not be forced into a

decision. We must look at it from all sides, for the good
of every one of us.

Guy is a strange, moody youth, given to sudden flashes
of great kindness and appearing to follow her rather
faithfully, and yet there is always the dark power of his
elder brother brooding over everything he does. Now he
says, it is typical of Hugh to give no thought to me. To
make no provision. How am I to live?

I shall give thought to you. Trust me. I was like a
lamb to the shearsman when I married your brother. I was
fifteen. I knew nothing although I thought I did. I was
besotted for a short while, a very short while, by Hugh's
chivalry. He seemed so manly, so brave, in his armour a
perfect knight, his need for me so overpowering, it tinged
our future with the magic of romance as the troubadours
sing of it until one day I saw him as he was and was in
despair, alone as I felt, in a sometimes hostile country,
but you were a lad of such restoring joy with your piping
and singing and your learning Welsh and making everyone
love to see you appear, like a sprite, turning from
English to Welsh before our very eyes, and so easy about
it, and how can you imagine now I will not make provision
for you?

Guy is quiet but is he consoled by her words?

I am twenty-two, she reminds. I am a widow. I have
rights. They say I will remarry. They say I am already
an object of desire to ambitious men. But do I want to be
beholden to any man again? Hugh was not the best of
husbands. You know that as well as I do.

Guy knows more than he should but now he gives one of
his quick smiles. Hugh never did learn Welsh, the sot-
wit. I doubt whether he was able to. All he knew was
fighting. It's ironic that he should die in some

16

unrecorded chevauchee in a godforsaken vill nobody has ever heard of. Typical of him. Unheroic to the last.

He echoes Hildegard's feelings but she gives him a reproving glance. We should not speak ill of the dead.

Guy bends his head but she catches the gleam of derision in his eyes. His brother had been a bully and baited his younger brother without mercy. She can see he is honestly glad he is gone and his sky empty of at least one lowering thunder cloud to darken his future.

With an expression that suggests agreement he says: he had no idea he would inherit anywhere in the Marches. His life was in the North, in England. He was shocked by what happened. The devious genealogy that brought him something so unlooked for as lands and a castle, he saw as a miracle from God. It meant he was chosen. It made him worse in his arrogance. That's why he went away, not because of you. He told me once, if he could split himself in two he would do so, but the lure of acquiring wealth from the French proved too strong and drove him off. He thought God would bless his greed because He had shown it was his right because he was the chosen one and whatever else he acquired was his by right also. He gives that easy smile. And now, of course, you're a subject of ambitious speculation. A widow possessing a third of her husband's estates is a prize to any shire knight. It is foregone, they say. You will remarry. That is what you will do. Our neighbour, the good Sir John, will find his lands conveniently augmented. He said if you choose him you will both prosper.

So he has said this to you too? The words follow closely what John has already said to her in private before setting out. We will both prosper, my lady. We will be a force in Wales on behalf of King Edward. From that will follow other prizes. We will both prosper.

17

Meanwhile, Westminster is awash with political discussions of the most violent kind. Swords are ordered to be left outside the doors of the Church where a prolonged debate is taking place. Guards are posted. Aware of danger, everyone looks about with narrowed eyes. Arrivals from the shires are still riding into town to take their places in the Chapter House where the Commons are gathering. These men come from every corner of the realm at King Edward's behest, from Berkshire, Shropshire, Essex and Kent, from the northern shires and from the south and west, Sussex is represented and the midlands, from all loyal shires come the sheriffs, the knights, the commoners, from the major towns come the burgesses, two from each, all those who may supply either from their own coffers or from taxation the gold the king needs to further his ambitions of conquest.

Grooms, pages, body servants and anyone who needs to earn a penny run in and out among the travel-stained from far-flung places, others come spry and rested, direct from comfortable city lodgings, carrying messages, greetings, reaffirming alliances and all from page to knight wearing the colours and blazon of some shire or other, some knight, some landholder, making the steps of the chapter house fill with a rainbow of colour, a gaudy shower of pigments, dyes, bleachings, gildings sufficient to dazzle the eye.

The London merchants are as lavish in appearance as their noble masters, adorned in fabrics of specialist weave straight from the Flemish looms, or in the silks of Lucca, in the brocades and organzas from Outremer, though some, deliberately tawny and dull of hue, draw attention to their sobriety to warn the money bags of the cautious to be opened only with proper cause, today offering probity, common sense and firmness of purpose against the dazzling corruptions of the royal court. These are the men to say no, this must stop. No, we will not finance any future follies. This must stop and we are the men to stop it. Our coffers are closed to you. And even more strongly, as it is later spoken aloud by the Commons in full agreement: King Edward must live off his own feudal rents, his own revenues, his own legitimate resources and not come begging to us to finance his dream of being crowned King of the French.

People of all levels, invited and uninvited, throng the doorway into the Chapter House to see them arrive, the first meeting convened to elect a leader, a man to speak on their behalf, to put their case to the lords, and to debate the matter in full in some other place where the council of the Commons may speak most privily before laying their demands for reform before the Lords. These matters are decided with speed and full agreement. Peter de la Mare, trusted and well-liked steward to the earl of March, is elected to speak for them all as prolocutor, as vaut-parler, chosen to address the nobility but content to keep them waiting until the Commons have come to agreement and thus they withdraw from the Chapter House to a more private nearby church where they can discuss their rebellion against the lackeys of the king and decide what they themselves, the Commons, the Shiremen and the burgesses and city merchants will accept and what they will not, without fear of death.

The crowds outside shout their suggestions for justice and an end to corruption through the open doors and when the doors are hauled shut they continue to shout advice to those within and chants are set up to drive the point home, tabors beating time, horns screaming to remind those privileged to sit inside that, if they fail, those outside are numerous enough to take matters into their own stout custody.

That they should threaten to fight in the streets! The shame of it!

Oh, heaven forfend!

Not in London!

Never here!

Don't be too sure. The soothsayers predict blood.

The confusion of opinion adds to Hildegard's personal quandary.

She returns to the hospitium and detains one of the lay brothers to ask after the child. Without speaking he points towards an inner chamber. Inside she sees several alcoves containing beds, some occupied, others not, and is met by non-committal faces when she enquiries after the girl. The Sister who rescued her from the street sits with bowed head beside a little cot on which a still form lies.

Hildegard approaches on soft feet. Is this Bet?

The nun halts in mid-prayer. Only look in, my lady. She is not to be disturbed.

The two smaller children are sitting in a huddle on the floor at the nun's feet, hiding in the black skirts of her habit. They do not move and only the boy glances up. He says nothing but his eyes, larger than ever, speak for him. His baby sister hides her face in his sleeve as if he can protect her from what is to come.

Have you had something to eat, my chicks? she whispers in a tone overcome by the stillness within the alcove where the cot is set.

The boy nods.

Both of you?

He nods again and tries to persuade his sister to raise her head, her hair a ball of fuzz like a dandelion clock, and two wide eyes looking out of a little face flushed with tears, a mute, sad, uncomprehending oval making Hildegard kneel down and take both children into her arms. They lean into her like little hounds.

A lay-sister appears and whispers in Hildegard's ear, they are well, both washed and fed and wearing garments newly laundered, though the boy's jerkin fell apart and we had to find a new one for him, too big but he'll grow into it. I can tell you nothing about Bet. She is not conscious though now she seems in little pain. We sat up all night, praying, doing what we could.

Has she spoken since I left you?

The lay-sister shakes her head. We thought she was sleeping but she will not wake. The infirmarer says it is best to allow her to rest undisturbed.

Hildegard looks down at the motionless features, small and dainty, with eyelashes fanning the pale cheeks, the lips as if carved prettily in ivory and but for the bruise and the dark badge of blood on the forehead, a face perfect, such as an angel might possess.

The lay sister touches Hildegard's arm. I'm sorry I have nothing more cheering to tell you.

Is there anything I might do?

Wait on God's will.

My gratitude for taking these waifs in.

We will take then permanently if need be and you so wish.

If it's best for them - ?

We think so. They are born and bred in the parish. It is our duty and pleasure to take them. Come again tomorrow.

I will.

21

As she leaves a prioress in the white robes of a Cistercian is being ushered inside by two monks who show her great deference even though she is not of their Order. But tears are already standing in Hildegard's eyes and she scarcely notices the new arrival through the sheen of moisture blurring them.

Later she tells Sir John about her visit and how there is no change in the girl's condition and then, seeing his flushed and excited expression, asks after the events in parliament.

It is all a furore of argument and counter-argument but not, he hastens to explain, on the topic of our main purpose. On that we are in full agreement. We are not an unguarded chest of gold to be filched by royal robbers. We all agree on that. We stand firm. But the detail, the detail of evidence against the embezzlers, this must be soundly brought, every document, deed, bill, account, all need to be perused by the clerks word by word to seal up every loophole and then the accused will be called to stand forth and be revealed for what they are. Can you believe this, Hildegard, his tone changes and he places a hand on her shoulder and leaves it there, friendly, no secret intention in his innocent gaze, can you believe Sir Richard Lyons has brought bills to the king for loans which were never made? Is it possible that men should do that? He and several others also agreed to buy back the king's debts - debts they themselves forced him to incur - at ridiculous rates of interest! Imagine forcing the king to pawn his royal crown and his best jewels to Lombardy bankers and then making a profit to release him from his debt! They are the necromancers of misfortune. He is too old, too senile and wallowed in lust for Madam Perrers to rouse himself sufficiently to see them for what they are.

It is up to us to strip away his blindfold, to reveal the truth about his ministers, his trusted advisors, his court thieves.

After this come days of turmoil which seem to lead only by slow moment after slow moment to the point when the Commons, swearing fealty to one another, are ready to stand as one, face to face with their over-lords in the Painted Chamber. The Commons have kept these lords, these dukes and earls, the men of royal lineage waiting seven days, seven days, while they discuss the levels of corruption and outright theft committed under the very nose of the king and in his name. Then lords Latimer, a northerner known to Hildegard by hearsay as a rapacious double-dealer, and Richard Lyons, Warden of the Mint, are summoned before the combined houses in parliament.

She, meanwhile, is unable to do more than present her plea of widowhood to an under-clerk, an assistant who is clearly burdened by the absence of a master with the more weighty matter of the impeachment of the king's ministers on his mind. Rubbing ink-stained knuckles over his face he asks her why she has not produced her husband's body to the proper authorities. This is a matter for the Coroner, he begins.

Forgive me, magister, there is no body –

No body? Then on what grounds do you claim a death has occurred?

My husband was fighting in a detachment in France under the command of the earl of Arundel and disappeared in a skirmish near a vill called…she fumbles for the piece of parchment she was given, reads out what it says.

The clerk flexes his fingers. This proves nothing. Without a body we cannot ascertain that a death has taken place. You must understand that. How else would we know he's dead? He may be a prisoner. How do we know that he may not be offered at some future date for ransom? We cannot rest a case on mere hearsay –

Two men came to me in my castle near Penarlag –

Is that one of Mortimer's strongholds?

No, although of course my husband supported Mortimer. He held the land in his own right as a bequest through the line matrilineal. It was proven. There is no doubt of his ownership.

I don't doubt your word but I must see the deeds.

I have them.

She hands some documents over and he flicks through them. Puts them to one side. And so, you say two men sought you out? What of it?

They brought verification of his death, two men from Brittany from the region where my husband is last known to have fought in a detachment of Arundel's militia. They handed me his ring and a document from a Breton captain recording his loss of ransom because of my husband's death. She hands both the ring and the document written in a spidery and almost illegible Breton to the clerk who purports to be able to read it - and maybe he can, she allows - which he then places on top of the deeds to Hugh's estate.

And what did they say to you, these two Bretons?

I was unable to understand them in any shared language but my steward speaks Welsh and between them they seemed to reach an agreement on the manner of Sir Hugh's death – It was from a wound sustained in battle.

My condolences but I must ask in all reasonableness is that all, their word and this? He rests a forefinger in the middle of the page.

What more can I give you?

I shall have to put the whole matter before my master. We shall need proof of your status, my lady. That might complete matters. Is there anyone who can speak for you?

A neighbour, Sir John Dinsdale. He will guarantee I am who I say I am.

The clerk relents a little and gives a flickering smile from behind the delicate haze of his fashionable beard. He steeples his fingers above propped elbows. You will understand that in this present situation your affairs will not be first in the queue? They will not take precedence over matters of state.

I understand that.

However, I can offer you a reasonable estimate that you will receive your widow's dower in due course and - he glances down at the unfamiliar name - your husband's property will be held in trust for your son. With another glance at the documents she has handed him, he adds, your son Bertrand, a child. He gives her a compassionate glance. You will continue to remain at your castle in the Marches until he is of age? He notices her uncertainty. Unless, he corrects, you are contemplating remarriage?

I have made no decision yet.

He begins to shuffle his writing materials into place. You are free to return now. Should anything unexpected arise from these, he taps the documents with one finger, you will be informed by the clerk of the court. He rises to his feet and offers a casual bow. I trust you have no further questions, my lady?

When she shakes her head, wondering how long she will have to wait for a decision, he adds, let Sir John come to me and make himself known to someone here in order to take his oath. I know him by sight. If you can extract him from his deliberations in the Commons committee I shall be pleased to see him. He hesitates and then, carefully he

says, these matters often take some time. With the
present parliament having no end in sight we clerks are
rushed off our feet. But take heart. You will eventually
get satisfaction.

Before Sir John can gather himself and put in an
appearance in front of the clerk of the court, something
terrible and unexpected happens. Prince Edward, the heir
to the throne dies.

The Commons, poised to put their demands, the barons
ranged in opposition, the city of London, the country
towns, the vills and hamlets of England, the farms, the
granges, the stables and workshops, the inhabitant of
every field and copse and royal forest, every man, woman
and bawling child old enough to understand, are halted in
their tracks and the entire realm is thrown into
confusion. Even while his father, the illustrious King
Edward III, struggles against old age, his warrior's body
wracked by weakness so that he can scarcely lift a cup to
his lips and in council has to be strapped upright in his
chair to pronounce the verdict whispered into his ear by
his concubine, Alice Perrers, even while this goes on, his
eldest son, the heir to the realm, famed and fabled
throughout Europe for valour and feats of arms, lying on
his stinking litter in a foul heap of rank flesh
relinquishes his soul to heaven.

And who is to rule next? The second son, duke Lionel,
is dead, poisoned, they say, by his father-in-law the duke
of Milan, or by some other ambitious devil. Or the third
son, vile Lancaster, duke John of Gaunt? Will it be him?

The people, lacking rights and privilege as they are,
will, even so, not accept that. Bill-hooks, scythes, axes
are remembered - and the whetstones with which to sharpen
them.

The Commons agree: we want no king called John.

An announcement is made. The old king made a whispered covenant weeks before with his now dead war hero son that the line of inheritance will not deviate from custom, the crown will pass through him, Prince Edward, to the prince's eldest son, the grandson of the present king. It will pass straight down the male line to young Richard. The boy will rule.

The chroniclers write it up and wipe their pens, a promise of fealty is made by the barons, and duke John of Gaunt, sufficiently cowed, devious or overcome with grief, third in line only, accepts the proposition, a boy king of ten will rule England, Ireland and as much of France as his grandfather could lay hold of in the fifty years of his war-mongering reign. A boy of ten. Richard. King.

Meanwhile Hildegard, the lady of the Marches, begins her wait on an answer regarding her own future from the clerks in their hive at Westminster Hall.

The dead prince, the valiant soldier, the one-time heir to the crown of England, lies in state in his castle at Berkhamstead with his previously written instructions now read aloud by his chamberlain on the manner of his funeral rites. He is to lie at Canterbury beside the tomb of Thomas a Becket, his body conveyed there by two destriers clothed in his arms of war and peace, with plumes and banners and all his devices and with his black pennant carried by an armed man alongside.

But before that his son, his heir, the royally sanctioned future king of England, young Richard who shall be the second of that name, is to be presented to the barons of England and to the newly formed and acknowledged Commons in order to make it clear who will rule next. Preparations from top to bottom of the realm begin at once, the markets thronging with the activities of weavers, broiderers, semptresses, gold and silver smiths, hat-makers, glovers and all guild workers involved with the proper presentation of the human form. Mercers do good business supplying all the trimmings that go with personal display. Sumptuary garments are inspected for infringements of the law. Fur brushed, leather polished, gold rubbed to its true dark lustre. A bother and a clutter as the wives preen, argument and nervous laughter following, then from every house the people set forth. There are some swift returnings for things forgotten. But the great setting out from all the palaces and towering houses and from the tenements near the wharfs and the stable yards and inns takes place and a cavalcade of the people converges on Westminster.

While they are in a frenzy of waiting for the prince to appear the lady of the Marches makes good use of her time and struggles through the assembling crowds to visit the girl who was struck down by Gaunt's careless militia, notes that there is still no change, that the nun who attends her is praying harder than ever and the hospitaller is shaking his head as he bends like a benign crow over the form lying on the cot. The best she can do is to take the two little ones off to a quiet corner and tell them a story. When one of the monks hands her a chap book she reads from that and when the boy asks about the patterns on the page she explains about letters and words and so the progress from illiteracy to literacy begins which she will pay the monks to further.

While she reads, a figure in Cistercian white appears in a doorway lit by the sun, a white flame burning through the Benedictine darkness, a shaft of brightness suggesting matters not of this world but of some unearthly visible realm seen only through the clear glass in the clerestory windows. And the flame flickers and remains motionless, splintering the darkness, standing in the midst of silence like a white flame dispelling the shadows and she, the prioress, blazes with white flame, and Hildegard is aware of the cold fire of the spirit, the silence, the power and the flame and feels it burn through the darkness and enter the chamber unrolling light before it.

The prioress says, I hear you are about to lose everything you possess?

She is drawn to her feet by the power of the flame and puts out a hand as if to warm it in a fire.

An exaggeration, domina. I trust it will never come to mean everything. Some things I would never want to lose until I lost the most precious gift of all.

Remember, lady, the things of this world are ephemeral but necessary. God be with you when you make your choice.

Sir John expresses a controlled interest in the progress of Hildegard's application to the courts and in the midst of the turmoil caused by the prince's death, the stunned grief, the fantasy of the funeral preparations when it seems his dark presence is still alive among them, the knight is assiduous enough to present himself that very morning before the clerks as guarantor, casual and confident that his lady of the Marches will gain everything owing to her and confident that he too will gain, step by step, what is owed her.

In conversation he invokes the law of Winchester against the Salic law the French espouse which, he says, seems to be based on a view that women cannot handle their own affairs and must therefore be deprived of them.

Later, when she leaves the abbey precinct and joins him near the great hall she observes his lips, very red and

29

mobile in the nest of his clipped black beard as he
speaks.

It is the basis of this infernal war with the French, he
repeats. It leads them to an intransigent refusal to
accept King Edward as their rightful king. Clearly he is
next in line. All laws say so except for the primitive
edict of Charlemagne which the French dukes insist on
merely in order to put one of their puppets on the throne.
Our kings are as French as theirs are, they speak French,
they read French, they even think in French. What does a
stretch of water between our two shores matter when it
comes to inheritance? Is King Edward not as good as the
nephew several degrees removed from their old king whom
they have foolishly set upon the throne? Now we even have
fellows in the Inns of Court trying to ride the same horse
through our own affairs but I tell you, my lady, I will
never allow you to be deprived of your inheritance.
Believe me, Hildegard, trust me and never fear. I am the
man to protect you.

I can think of no good reason why Bertrand should not
inherit his father's land nor any reason why I should not
be allowed to stand as guardian and run things in trust
until he is of age, should I so wish.

That was not the same as inheriting outright and she
knows it. She is also aware that Sir John imagines that he
himself could assume the right for her and rule her domain
and is therefore the more keen to secure it on her behalf.
There is never a moment when she is not aware of this.

Should you so wish? He looks askance. His red mouth
hangs open. I trust you do so wish, my dear, otherwise we
are here in vain.

She goes into the Lady Chapel for the purposes of
contemplation. The silence is like a globe, swelling,

immanent with mystery. Light falls in shafts of colour over the mosaic floor, on the gold of lectern, candelabra and on the leather marker tooled in gold leaf hanging from the open book. Stillness. Silence. A rich scent of incense. She sinks into it, allows her thoughts to rearrange themselves. She believes that Sir John's ire on her behalf may well be in vain.

She sees that should she lose what he imagines to be her right this will not suit her marriage prospects with him one bit. Her dowry is something she will fight for, but the land, against the natural right of her son? The thought of marriage is becoming less attractive when she considers all that she will lose. She is no burgess's wife who could take her husband to court at little expense should they have a disagreement. Such land and property as she might hold in her own name would incur the rapacity of the legal profession and she would be left with the lees after they had ridden their horses at full gallop through their law books as Sir John fears. Is she ready to give up her glimpse of freedom so soon?

A flame burns steadily behind a screen and she lifts her eyes to the high window where the circle of blue framed within it opens onto infinity.

With no sign yet of the little prince's arrival she returns to the abbey yard. The sound of singing from one of the chantries floats on the air, each note like a shard of silver as a flame of white appears, the prioress, with hands inside her sleeves, her serenity unaltered when her glance falls on Hildegard, calls, Join us, my lady. Why not?

There is tranquillity in her progress, and a group of nuns emerge from a nearby door, six, walking two by two in black, and the one gleaming, ethereal, in their wake, and it is like balm to Hildegard's troubled thoughts to follow them, blinded, uncertain, towards the close dark of the shrine with the words why not? chiming in her ears throughout the ritual that follows. Why not join us? Is that what the prioress meant? Join us. Why not? She meant merely 'follow' surely? But something more opens up. *Why not?*

Images in the high windows of painted glass suggest the lives of other women and what they had made of a monastic life, the famed Abbess of the Whitby Benedictines, Hild, for instance, mistress of a double house, convenor of the Great Synod that set the date for Easter, and also her own namesake, Abbess Hildegard, advisor to Popes and prolific writer and music maker at Bingen, and Abbess Eloise of the Paraclete, defying the condemnation of Bernard of Clairvaux and the excommunication of her lover and mentor Peter Abelard, and Catherine of Siena, an advisor to another Pope in Rome and to the bellicose dukes of Tuscany. *And why not?* They were all women of power. And at home are the mystics, Julian of Norwich, drawing people to her for advice and solace, assuaging the sorrows of the poor and dispossessed, and of course all the many abbesses in charge of land, farm stock, granges, all contributing to the wealth of the realm, running their convents, priories and abbeys as well as, and in many cases, better than men, and the hundreds of self-effacing but no less effective nuns providing schools and hospitals for the poor. *And why not?* How could she believe there was no answer to the question? The answer stood clear, like a challenge. Even my own name, she reminds herself superstitiously, even that suggests a course I might follow. *And why not?*

But I'm no mystic, she decides through the rituals of kneeling and praying and lifting her voice to join the

voices of the others, with the lancets allowing in a
dazzle of coloured light, the reds, the blues and yellows
seeming to dissolve the worn stones while the joined
voices melt into the empyrean, and underneath this, still
the objection to why not because she cannot see herself as
an advisor to anyone and at present can only think of
tending this one, poor injured child and her nestlings and
others, sick and put-upon, the lost and alone. Heaven
knows there are enough starving orphans in the world who
need help until they can help themselves, she thinks. I
will have wealth enough when I am granted my dowry to buy
a place in one of the Orders, with the Benedictines, or
the Cistercians, or one of the other orders, and I might
return to my home county and ask to be taken in as a lay-
sister even.

The more she thinks about it, however, the more
impossible it seems. She has no vocation and has always
enjoyed worldly pleasures and accepts the fact without
struggle, abhorring the thought of struggling to come to
something she cannot accept with her mind, something
against the world she perceives through her senses. She
is too rational to succumb to the voluptuousness of magic,
to that laziness and ease of acceptance of the obviously
impossible. She is too recalcitrant, too vain-glorious,
would find the discipline hateful, the ritual trying, and
the inability to say what she thinks untenable. It is not
for me, she decides. But then again, nor is marriage.

A memory of Hugh's rough usage when he was the only one
to take pleasure in the carnal acts permitted by the
Church returns and no contemplation of it will dispose of
this objection. Even with a more kindly lord every wish
or need would be proscribed and she would have to yield
her rights and if she did not yield she would have to
fight for her self-esteem against the rapacity of the men-

33

at-law. But, she tells herself again, I have no vocation
for the alternative. My doubts would lead me into all
kinds of trouble. I cannot accept that the body and blood
of Christ is turned into bread and wine as if by an act of
magic. I cannot accept this. William Wyclif, with his
close reading of the scriptures also cannot accept it and
nor can many clear-sighted and common-sensical fellows and
down-to-earth housewives nor practical Guildsmen, nor many
of the nobility who do not believe in magic either. What
we see is what there is and what there is is all we see.
This is a knot I cannot unpick.

What she saw next when she left the precinct were the
massive crowds gathering to witness the arrival of the
golden boy, ten year old Richard of Bordeaux, the hope of
all the country, at the great doors of Westminster Hall
and on this fair day at the end of June he rides between
the houses along the narrow streets crammed with cheering
citizens, cheers that greet him in a ground swell of grief
and love bursting from the throats of every man, woman and
child, whose hopes for salvation have been ignored. What
she hears in the roar that greets him is a cry for
validation from people who feel they have no voice, no
hope, a cry of trust that this royal child will bring them
to the gates of heaven itself and dissolve their grief.
     It is right that he is a gentle boy of great beauty,
that he wears his gold-encrusted silk with dignity, that
he is seen to be kind to his little white horse, polite to
the adults who guard him and when in the tumult of
adoration he arrives at the doors of the great and ancient
hall it is right that he allows himself to be ushered
briskly towards his future so that he has to quicken his
pace to keep up with his guards, a good-natured smile on
his face and then a shy halting at the threshold before

making his first appearance before his vassals, the barons.

He is seen by those standing nearest to slip his hand into that of his mother Joan, the Princess of Wales, the Fair Maid of Kent, widow of the Black Prince, daughter-in-law to aged King Edward, and by her side he steps over the threshold into the hall for his presentation to be greeted by a monstrous roar.

All hail! And hail the future king!

And as one the nobility kneel before him and the thunder of steel armour on stone echoes and re-echoes like an endless wave echoing and reverberating round the great vault of Westminster with a sound like doom.

She imagines her little son Bertrand being brought before the household in the Marches, older than at present, and aware of the task before him, the balance he would have to bring to the nervous factions of the settlers and the settled and by chance she glances down the hall towards the place where Gaunt, Duke John, is standing in a line with his two living younger brothers, his expression vague, yet eyes dark with a sneering contempt as he nurses his jealousy and ambition for absolute power. The clipping of his wings by the Commons during these last few weeks has changed things, a difference in his manner has become apparent, his brusqueness is smoothed to a civility that sits strangely on what was his former self. Is it to be trusted, this amelioration? Something about his absence now, his aura of absence, of detaching himself while his thoughts fly elsewhere suggests that the battle with the Commons is not conceded by either side.

Even though Speaker de la Mare might get all he asks for, laws brought in, fraudsters imprisoned, the mistress dismissed, as soon as the Commons separate to return to

35

their castles in the shires, to their distant towns, he could easily slip back and re-inhabit his old desire and ambition to do what he can to reverse the laws about to be enacted now. He seems to her like a man who is patiently biding his time.

Someone stands beside her in the crowd, a whisper comes: will he reverse the laws of the Commons as soon as they return to their homes? With her misgivings read so accurately, she turns to find the prioress beside her, sardonic mouth tilted in a private smile, who adds: isn't that the question everyone fears to ask?

The herald calls for those in favour of a future King Richard to cry, Aye! The roof timbers shake. Dust flies down from the purlins.

Gaunt, as head of the Council, steps forward to reply but what he says is inaudible. When he strides solemnly between the ranks of standing militia following the chair bearing his father King Edward, he gestures for a group of his own men to come with him and approaching the doorway where Hildegard is standing he scatters the onlookers so that they are pressed back on themselves with mutters and dark looks and she can almost touch him, his arm encased in steel within a hand's breadth of where she stands, and as he sweeps everyone aside she hears his order to his captain of guards, Attend me with six others.

In a close-pressed group the men exit to wild cheers for the aged king as soon as the doors are flung open followed by a falling silence at the sight of the duke and he passes between them with his men, his armed men, in a black silence. His grooms are straightaway hurrying forward with his destrier and as he is offered a knee by which to vault into the saddle a lone catcall from the back of the crowd is heard. It brings a gust of laughter, sharp as rain and quickly quelled, and from Gaunt himself

the same blank face with which he listened to the eulogies
pouring forth onto the grey head of the king his father
and onto the fair young head of the king to be, his
nephew, the child Richard.

And as he clatters out of the yard with his entourage in
close guard about him, the prioress pulls at Hildegard's
linen sleeve and says, follow me, my lady, if you will.

Imagining there is news about the injured child and with
the crowds now pouring from the hall she is swept away
after her, away from the thick of the crowds until they
reach the empty cloisters. The prioress comes to a halt.

Now sit awhile and talk to me.

I see we are both northerners, Hildegard begins. She falls
silent, too many words block and jostle to take form.

I suspected that about you when I saw you run into the
road despite the steel-shod boots of the militia. Go on.

And Hildegard haltingly begins to outline her dilemma.

The prioress gazes off across the cloister to a fountain
making a flickering show of rainbows in the summer
sunlight and when Hildegard comes to the difficulty of
admitting to her thoughts in the Lady Chapel - the strange
answer that had come to her question why not? - the
prioress continues to watch them while saying helpfully,
there are many of us down here in London, we folk from the
north. We come here to do what we must. We taste this
life in the great city and find great pleasure and purpose
in it but after a time we begin to feel a great longing to
return home. When you feel like that, come to us.

Where are you? Hildegard asked.

My priory is near the north bank of the Humber in
Haltemprice. It's remote but we have a useful community
of monks only a few miles across the marsh at an abbey
called Meaux. Up there in the East Riding it's a country

of big skies, freedom, a certain harsh purity. Either you like it or you don't. Much depends on whether you have the spirit to engage with such austerity. She gives her a frank stare. My priory stands on a wooded hill above an ancient Saxon vill called Swyne. No men. You'll find that difficult. No fashionable gowns. She eyes Hildegard's crimson mantle. Little meat, but plentiful fish, good wine, vegetables we can grow, orchard and hedgerow fruits, and passionate cooks who make the most of it all. Frugality is the watch-word. Definitely that. But there is in that place all one needs. We leave our 'wants' at the door. Austerity, certainly that in our day-to-day lives, I would never say otherwise. Much joy though. Light. Space. Serenity. All the colours of the seasons. The rhythm of the land. Happiness in small things.

But I have no belief. Only ones that might be seen as heresy and I would not wish that on your community.

You only need believe in what we do, in its necessity, its rightness, its value. Without us many folk would live in a state of loss and never see the light. You settled those little ones well, you might do the same for others like them.

I did nothing and what I did came down to payment, my worldly good fortune.

The prioress gives a snort of laughter. We are the wealthiest Order in England. We are wool producers. We export. We have set our quay by the river so that we can trade with Flanders and into Tuscany and beyond. We are not women to sit gossiping and doing nothing in petty obscurity. We are merchants and a force in the world. Why am I here in Westminster at this time? Because our power is sought by those who wish to increase their own. We are vital to the survival of the realm. You will know about wool in Wales, I should think? You know about the business side of it?

Yes. Our shepherds run many sheep over those hills.

She thinks of them at this moment as those hills, those distant hills, more distant than when measured in miles. It's true she could be useful in this place by the Humber, this priory south of Castle Hutton with, as it happens, only the long leagues of the wildwood between them. The simplicity of the prioress's way of talking about her life appeals, but a world without men? No romance, no love of the physical kind she craves? Could she ever live a life like that? Her thoughts fly to Ulf. It would never be possible to do more than think of him with unfulfilled longing wherever she was because she could not marry a steward, Lord Roger would never allow it and even if Ulf had ever thought of such a thing, by now he was probably betrothed. Even so, there might be other men. They would not all be like Sir John, desiring her land above herself.

The prioress pleated one of her sleeves in absent-minded thought then smoothed it out again. I travel northwards in a few week's time with quite a retinue as usual, but plenty of room for more. Bring your children to travel with us so they can have a look at Yorkshire and you can find out how your Welsh flocks get on without you. Your young brother-in-law will, of course, remain at home to over-see matters, a young man with a useful destiny, I would think...? With that she rises to her feet and swiftly crosses the yard.

Hildegard sits on for some time with a tumbled heap of thoughts that need carding, spinning and eventually weaving into a pattern that makes sense.

Look! he says. For you! A flurry of crimson flies into her lap. Ribbons. They run through her fingers like

39

silk. They *are* silk. The finest silk from Lucca. A gift before we leave London! His eyes are dancing.

A gift? But what's it for, Guy?

It's for you! He stands square-legged before her, thumbs in his belt, beaming, the beginnings of a beard he has been trying to grow looking thicker today as his boyish fairness darkens. It makes him suddenly handsome and more knightly.

But why for me? They're lovely but I haven't done anything to deserve presents.

He sits down beside her and she has to move along the bench to make space. I went into the city with those bowmen I've been practising Welsh with. They wanted to get ribbons for their sweethearts at home. I thought…he glances quickly away and back. I thought they'd look very fine woven into your hair.

They're beautiful. She threads one of the ribbons through her fingers and seeing what she is doing he places his own fingers in the alternate loops so that their hands are tied palm to palm.

Hand-fast, he says, looking into her eyes without smiling.

She laughs out loud. Sot wit! She is laughing like a girl but when she catches sight of his expression she falters and before she can speak he gets up, colour racing across his face as after a slap.

Guy!

He is heading rapidly towards the door.

Guy, wait! I have a gift for you too.

He turns. For me?

Not a gift exactly but some change that I hope will please you so that you may come to see it as gift in the future.

You're talking in riddles, my lady.

40

He comes to kneel on the floor at her feet, untrustful now, his defences up.

I have decided to take the children up to Yorkshire, to show them what it's like. I am asking you to oversee matters at home. You might find you enjoy being lord of a Marcher domain.

You'll leave me in charge?

With Gwylim to be heeded if a conflict arises, yes. Will you oblige me by doing this for me?

Hildegard? I cannot believe it. I thought you saw me as incompetent, just as Hugh did?

Never. I could always see through his needling. His continual criticism was obvious for what it was, deliberate malice. I know you to be perfectly as you should be at your age, a fine horseman, a fearsome archer, maybe something of a wild Welsh man…She pushes his shoulder with her beribboned fingers. Prove to me you can do it and that Hugh was wrong?

He grips her hand, ribbons and all, crushing them. Dear Hildegard. I solemnly plight my troth.

Parliament has resumed its inexorable course with the Commons gaining the upper hand for the first time in history, fraudsters impeached, made to pay back what they stole, and sent to the Tower, the king's whore removed from his fond and foolish presence.

Sir John, casting his vote with his fellow Commoners, has seen them victorious, has tasted the power they possess when they stand together and speak out. England will never be the same, he tells Hildegard. These are ten weeks to change our freedoms forever.

He has with him today his stag hound, an enormous lymer, a silent creature that can bring down a man within a few yards such is its speed and purpose. It reminds Hildegard of Sir John, somehow, his focussed aim when hunting down his prey, his apparently placid demeanour otherwise. Now she is to thwart him and escape him she wonders what he will do. She tells him of her plan.

Northwards? And then back to Wales, surely?

It is my home at present. I shall go and collect the children and…a glance at the lymer, and I shall fetch my two hounds with me, for hunting and protection and then, who knows, by then we should have an answer from the courts about my dowry and Bertrand's inheritance.

That lymer of yours, Duchess as you call her, was sired by this fellow here. He fondles the head of his hound. I gave her to Hugh as a pup as soon as he set foot in Wales. You'll be needing a good hound, I told him. The fool should have taken her to France. And the other one, the little brindled one, Bermonda, you'll be taking her too, will you? He nods as if it all makes sense. And that is all he has to say about her going away. Maybe he believes she will change her mind and never set forth. Maybe he believes she will eventually succumb to his blandishments?

Guy insists that he can quite easily go and fetch the children himself. His new bowmen friends are going back. He'll go with them and return with the children and their nurse-maid in a char, he says. You can wait here in Westminster for news from the courts. Hildegard is relieved not to have to return in case she is persuaded to change her mind after all. You are so thoughtful, Guy. She gives him a kiss on the cheek. He tells her he will be back in under a week.

The little injured child called Bet who only wanted to beg bread from duke John for her brother and sister eventually opens her eyes in a bewildered way and looks round to see the nun sitting in vigil beside her cot. By the time Guy returns with the children from Wales she is beginning to walk again and the five are seen here and there like sprites within the precinct. They are followed at a distance by a stately hound and a lively little table dog who gets under everyone's feet.

And so it is, at the beginning of July the Good Parliament at last comes to an end. It is one of the longest on record. The Commons win all their demands and there is great rejoicing from those who feel relief at an end to the wasteful plunder of their resources by the corrupt ministers surrounding the king and triumph that at last they have won their point. It is the first time in the history of the realm that the independent voice of the Commons has been heard and obeyed. It is also the voice of ordinary people who have no say in the laws that govern their lives. They call it the Good Parliament and sing songs in celebration of their new found power.

It is over and the crowds are dispersing. The yard outside the palace of Westminster is emptying. The prioress, her baggage-train and her many followers are on the move. Hildegard says farewell to Guy and Sir John then joins the train with her children and her hounds. On a fine day at the end of July she sets out on the journey north that will change her life forever.

As for the achievements of the Commons, it is predicted by the Westminster soothsayers that when everyone has gone home to the shires, John of Gaunt will make sure that most of their gains are lost. And so begins the long and bitter battle for the Crown of England.

f you like detection and adventure set in a firm historical context, or imply want to read more about Hildegard and her times you can see my ebsite www.cassandraclark.co.uk where you can also find out about the seven books in the series from **Hangman Blind** to **The Scandal of the Skulls.** Most are published by St Martin's Press but you can download all of them as ebooks. The eighth in the series - **The Alchemist at Netley Abbey** - is already in first draft and Hildegard herself can be followed @nunsleuth where you'll find more snips and bits about her medieval world. Happy reading!

Printed in Great Britain
by Amazon

42601325R00030